A ROMANCE FOR CHRISTMAS

Kayelle Allen

www.romancelivesforeverbooks.com

DISCLAIMERS

This eBook is a work of fiction. Names, characters, and incidents depicted in this book are products of the author's imagination, or are used in a fictitious situation. Any resemblances to actual events, locations, organizations, incidents or persons – living or dead – are coincidental and beyond the intent of the author.

To request permission for quotes and for all other inquiries, contact the author via email at kayelle.allen@yahoo.com or her website http://kayelleallen.com

DEDICATION

This book is dedicated to my sister Cherry in memory of Bill. A special thank you to my critique partners -- your encouragement means everything.

Chapter One

"Mommy?" Christine's young voice broke in on her thoughts.

Dara put down the romance she'd been re-reading, the favorite she'd had since she was sixteen. She'd sold all her others at a yard sale the previous week. "What is it, sweetie?"

"Why don't we has a real tree for Chribmas?"

"Why don't we 'have'," she corrected. "Come sit by me." Dara patted the couch and tucked her chenille robe closer around her.

One arm around Matilda, her cloth doll, Christine climbed up beside her mother and cuddled.

Matilda's going to need stuffing before long. Her head flopped forward, face against her flat chest. *When did the lace on her dress get so ragged?* Dara smoothed the doll's dress. "Remember when Daddy went home to heaven before Christmas last year?"

Christine knuckled her eyes and yawned. "I 'member."

"And then Mommy got hurt in the car accident and couldn't go to work?"

"Uh huh."

Dara took a deep breath. "Well, it meant there was no money for a real tree this year. But I'm sure Santa will still bring you presents." Gifts Dara bought by selling her entire collection of romance novels at a yard sale at her friend Sherilyn's house. "And we drew a tree, right?" She pointed at the crayon-bright drawing taped to the wall. Construction paper ornaments decorated each branch.

"But it doesn't smell like a Chribmas tree."

Dara hugged her. "I know, baby. I know."

"How will Santa leave his presents?" Christine pulled away and got on her knees. "He can't put them under the tree, Mommy."

"Oh, honey!" She ruffled her daughter's hair, swallowing the lump in her throat. "Santa will find a way." She leaned forward and kissed her little girl. "We should get you in bed so he can come. He can't leave presents while you're awake."

She followed her daughter into her room, got her tucked into bed and sat beside her, stroking her golden hair. Christine gazed up at her from under thick dark lashes. Her deep-blue eyes never failed to remind Dara of her late husband.

Jack had been Dara's high school sweetheart. Tonight marked a year and nine days since the accident that had claimed his death. Neither she nor Jack had family other than each other. His coworkers knew, and they'd helped that first year, bless them. His senseless death happened right before Christmas. What if something happened to her too? As an orphan herself, Dara experienced fear and anxiety for her daughter. Tears of loneliness, terror of the future, of raising her daughter without Jack at her side. Anger at everything and everyone. At his company for sending him on the trip. At Jack for going. Guilt for feeling angry ate at her.

The night Jack had left, they'd argued over it and he'd slammed the door when he left. But then he'd stopped the car halfway down the drive, gotten out, and had come back inside to kiss her and tell her he regretted having to go, but that he had to. He promised he'd be back before Christmas. They'd shared a long, cherishing kiss and she'd waved until he was out of sight.

Six hours later, his plane went down over the Gulf of Mexico in a freak storm. All on board were lost.

More guilt and doubt set in with the New Year. Things she should have said. Should have done. Why had she let him go? Why had God allowed her child to grow up without a father?

Her friend Sherilyn had walked through it all at her side, helping her get a job, watching Christine, being there when all Dara needed was to cry. This year, the company had forgotten Jack and the family he left behind. So much for "The Company with Families at Heart." Jack's insurance had paid off the house, and there was enough money to survive for a few months. While looking for a job, she'd sold furniture, her good silver, and pawned all her jewelry, except her wedding ring.

Dara rubbed her face with both hands, willing herself to hold on for her daughter's sake. To be strong. To be both mother and father. Women had done it for centuries. They'd survived. So would she.

"Mommy?" Christine rubbed Dara's arm. "Read me the story about the mouse that's quiet."

"That's a great story. My mother used to read it to me when I was little." Dara snuggled beside her, and opened her daughter's favorite Christmas book. At least she'd been able to give her the gift of reading. When Jack had been alive, he'd always made sure there was money for books. She would miss her own collection, but at least Christine would have something from Santa. "'T'was the night before Christmas..."

After Christine drifted off to sleep, Dara pushed off the bed. She was gaining strength daily, and would finish therapy the first week of January and return to work. Disability paid for the basics - lights, phone, water, trash collection, and she'd never bought anything on credit, refusing to dig herself into a hole she'd never escape once it got started.

It'll be great to have a full income again! I wish it could have come in time for Christmas.

She went to the closet and pulled down a box with a ball, crayons, paper, and three books. Sherilyn had brought over a few things as well. This wasn't the grand Christmas that Dara had wanted for Christine, but Dara had already sold her other valuables. There was nothing left but her wedding ring.

She didn't wear it. Removing it had been part of saying good-bye to Jack.

Sherilyn had said it would help, and it had. Sort of. But not much.

Dara sank into one of the kitchen chairs and put her face in her hands.

Sometime later, when the doorbell rang, she grabbed a paper towel and dried her eyes. The clock over the stove said nine o'clock. Who would be calling at this hour on Christmas Eve? She stuffed the wet towel in her robe pocket on the way to the door.

The peephole showed a policeman in a crisp black uniform, wearing one of those Smokey Bear hats. It took her back to the night Jack had died. She unlatched the door and opened it an inch, dread tightening her chest.

"Oh, my God. Is something wrong, Officer?"

"No, ma'am." He removed his hat. His smile showed sparkling white teeth and a shock of bright blond hair that fell over his brow. "I'm Scott Gregori. My daughter Susan and your Christine are in the same preschool class. I don't suppose you remember me. I was at your husband's funeral last year."

In a flash, she remembered him.

Their daughters' preschool was part of a small church. The school had sent a notice that the mother of one of their students had passed away, along with suggested ways to discuss the death of a loved one with children. Dara had attended his wife's funeral to pay her respects. When Jack died, only about a month later, Scott had come to pay his.

Unlike Jack, Officer Gregori had brown eyes. Her heart fluttered in a way it hadn't since--

Instantly ashamed of herself for such a visceral reaction, she clutched her robe against her throat. "Oh, yes. I remember. Please, won't you come in?" She opened the door wider.

"I brought you and Christine something." He bent down and picked up an oversized box before stepping inside. "This morning, I heard about your accident, and I thought-- Well, maybe you could use some help with Christmas presents for your daughter." He added, "If you wouldn't mind."

Dara shut the door behind him. "It'll make Christine happy, and that's what counts. You're so kind to do this."

He waved off her thanks with a quick gesture and set down the box. "All of us at the station chipped in and I went shopping. We figured money was tight so we wanted you to have this." He handed her a fat envelope.

She opened it, gasped and covered her mouth. A pile of twenties, tens, fives and ones filled it. "Oh. Oh, my-- my goodness."

He was smiling. "We all have families, and we help each other when things--" He swallowed. "Anyway, you know how it is in a town this size. We watch out for each other. The crew at the station and I wanted you to have that. And don't try to refuse." He set a hand over hers. "All of us have been there. Use it however you need."

Shaking, she refolded the envelope with extreme care. Words wouldn't come. She slid it into her pocket. "Thank you," she whispered, tears blurring her vision.

"The cop who filed the police report on your accident is my cousin, which was how I heard about your accident. I saw the papers on it when he filed the final report today and recognized your name. He finally caught the guy who hit your car."

She clasped her hands. "He caught him?"

"Sure did." He reached into the box. "He was insured, so you'll probably end up getting a good-sized settlement." He held up a stuffed dog as big as her daughter. "Where would you like me to put these toys?"

"Oh!" Dara grabbed the wet paper towel from her pocket and wiped her eyes. Happy tears this time. Unable to speak, she gestured toward the paper Christmas tree.

Officer Gregori unloaded the biggest pile of toys she'd ever seen. Christmas morning was going to be such fun, watching Christine realize "Santa" had indeed found a way. That would make Dara's entire day.

When he finished, he smiled at her, hat in hand. "There's one more thing in this box. I know you're going to think I'm some kind of sap, but--"

"I think no such thing! I think you're the most wonderful Santa I've ever seen." Dara blushed at the blurted confession, and they both shared an embarrassed laugh.

"I'm more like an elf, actually. Santa sent me to help you, that's all."

Dara smiled at that. "Please. Show me what's in the box."

"Well, my wife used to read a lot, and I never had the heart to give her books away. I stopped by my house and picked some up. I thought maybe you'd like to have them." He tipped the box on its edge and showed her.

All of them were romance novels.

When she started crying, he helped her to a chair. "I'm sorry. I didn't mean to make you sad."

"Not sad," she squeaked. "Happy. Romance-- it's my favorite." She grabbed another paper towel and wiped her eyes and nose. "This is the nicest Christmas I've ever had."

He sat in the chair nearest her. "I'm glad I could help."

She wiped her eyes again. "Could you maybe-- Could you stay for some coffee, Officer Gregori?"

"Please, call me Scott." He set his hat on the table. "I'm off work and Susan's all tucked in at my mother's. We've spent Christmas Eve there since Susan was born. I can stay long enough for coffee."

She got up and put on the kettle as Scott stretched his long legs. the chocolate brown of his eyes was fringed by thick lashes. He gave her a slow smile.

Is he flirting with me? Her heart made another little flutter and took wing. She pulled down two mugs with candy canes decorating them. *Don't be silly, Dara! Ten minutes ago you were crying over Jack. It's Christmas, that's all. Don't go reading things into people's gestures of kindness.*

She turned back to Scott. "I don't have decaf, and it's so late. I have a couple of herbal tea bags left. Would you prefer those? I don't want to keep you awake all night."

Scott licked his lips and then smiled, as if thinking of some private joke. "I'll probably need that caffeine. I bought Susan a three-wheeled cycle and I still have to put it together, and Mom always needs help getting the turkey into the oven. She starts it at midnight. Says if it cooks slow overnight it's so moist it--" He sat up straight. "Say, what are your plans for Christmas dinner?"

"What?" She turned so quickly she dropped a spoon and stooped to pick it up, her face going hot when she realized it exposed her bare legs. Rising carefully, she wrapped her robe tighter and tied the belt in a double knot before getting out a clean spoon. It wouldn't do for him to see her threadbare nightie.

Scott played with the brim of his hat. "I'd like it if you'd come over and have dinner with my family. My mother would love it."

"Thank you, Scott, but I'm sure your mother wouldn't appreciate two extra guests at the table unannounced."

He dismissed the argument with a wave of his hand. "Mom will be thrilled. I won't take no for an answer. She'll enjoy meeting Christine. She keeps Susan while I work and having Christine over will keep both girls busy. Besides, I promise, Mom makes the best turkey you've ever had." He leaned closer as if sharing a secret. "And my dad will bless you for saving him from eating it for the next solid week." He winked.

"Are you sure?"

Scott tapped his badge. "On my honor. I'll pick you up at noon. Dinner's always promptly at three, and the girls can spend some time together. We adults can have some coffee, or my mom's spiced tea, and talk."

She ducked her head, nodding. "Okay. We'll be ready." The big stuffed dog fell over, catching her attention.

"I'll fix it." Scott crossed the room, and bent over to right the dog and prop him against the wall.

Dara swallowed at the sight of that tight body and long, hard legs inside his uniform. She fanned her face and turned back to the coffee. *What would Jack think of me lusting after another man?*

She took a deep breath, and remembered her friend Sherilyn's words. *Jack's gone, Dara. He'd want you to be happy. He'd want you to go on. Your happiness was always what he wanted.*

She poured hot water over the coffee crystals and stirred each cup. "It's ready." She carried the cups to the table and set one in front of Scott. "How do you like it?"

Their gazes met and held. He gave her that mischievous smile of his that made her wonder what he was thinking.

"Black's fine." He sipped the coffee. "This is good."

"I'm sorry I don't have anything more than instant."

"It's what I use at home. Never could get the hang of all those filters and timer settings and the fancy espresso attachment thingy. My mom has to have everything just so, and so did my wife." He shrugged, broad shoulders filling out that uniform in a way that made Dara's mouth go dry. "To me, coffee is coffee. This is my brand. I hate that slop at the station. Always tastes like someone strained it through gym socks." He grimaced. "Now this," he held up the cup. "This is coffee worth drinking."

"Thank you." She reached behind her for the other chair and sank into it. She cleared her throat and sat up straighter, hands folded before her on the table, trying to think of something intelligent to say. "Um, what department are you in, Scott?"

He finished his sip of coffee. "It's a new one. We're trialing an old-fashioned way of patrolling downtown."

"New, but it's old?"

His grin could melt butter. She pulled the chenille robe tighter. *Focus, Dara.* She measured her breaths, trying not be affected by his physical appeal.

"There are six of us who walk downtown. The beat was strictly volunteer basis. The six of us on the station track team went for it. It builds up muscle and gives us an advantage when we compete regionally."

"A leg up, huh?"

Scott chuckled. "Good one. You got it."

"I used to run track in high school. Haven't been running in years. My leg is better now. I can walk normally, but maybe running -- a little -- would help me." She considered the cost of running shoes. "After I'm working again. Maybe I can start running on weekends."

Scott finished his coffee. "Call me and I'll go with you. There's a great park on the other side of town that's built for runners." He pulled a card out of his pocket and wrote on the back. "There are mile markers and workout equipment. Places to stop and stretch, and good fountains so you won't dehydrate. Here." He handed her the card.

A policeman's official card, it showed contact info and email, an abuse hotline number and the seal of the city. Dara turned it over. In bold print, he'd written "cell" followed by his number.

When she met his gaze, the intensity in his eyes sent a flush of heat over her. She mumbled her thanks, too tongue-tied by his smile to form full words.

"There's a new class for novice runners forming sometime in January. My department's involved in coaching it. Part of our community involvement initiative. Why don't you give me your number? I can let you know when the class opens."

She picked up one of her business cards from the desk and brought it to him. "My cell's on the right."

"Thank you. And thanks for the coffee. It's been great to sit down and talk like this. I haven't had a chance since my wife--" He cleared his throat. "I'd like to do this again sometime. Maybe Susan and Christine would like to go for ice cream between now and New Year's and we could talk."

"Oh, I'd love that, and so would Christine." Dara pressed a hand to her chest.

"Good, then." He picked up his hat, and brushed lint from it, not meeting her gaze right away. "Maybe two days after Christmas?"

Dara nodded. "I'd love it."

Scott stood. "Thank you, Dara."

"No, thank *you*." Dara stood. "I can't tell you what all this means to Christine and me." Afraid she'd give in to her impulse and hug him, she wrapped her arms around herself. When he held out his hand, she slid hers into it, suddenly aware of her peeling pink nail-polish. She hadn't even noticed. Had he? Her cheeks felt warm.

"Dara." Scott clasped her hand in both of his and simply held it. "I know this has been a hard year for you, because it's been hell for me without my wife. I want you to know it's going to be all right. We have iron-clad evidence against the guy who hit you, and I'm going to do everything I can to give you and your little girl a great Christmas. I don't want you to worry about that." He lifted her hand and kissed it. "I'll see you tomorrow."

Tears filled her eyes. Moved by this man's inner strength, touched beyond measure by his compassion, she stood there, unable to speak.

Scott opened the door and paused to look back. "Make sure you lock this." He patted the door, popped on his hat and smiled that devastating smile of his. "Good night." He went out and closed the door.

Dara hurried over and put one eye up to the peephole.

Scott was standing there as if waiting for something.

She flipped the locks.

He nodded with satisfaction and almost danced down the front steps, whistling as he crunched through the snow to his car.

"Wow." She leaned back against the door. Joy filled her. Had Christmas ever felt so good? The season when magic happened. She hurried to the phone to call Sherilyn. When she answered, Dara didn't even let her say hello. "Sheri! Did you know there's a six-foot tall, blond elf on the police force? Wait till I tell you what's happened!"

Chapter Two

Scott whistled all the way to his mom's house, grabbed his overnight case out of the trunk, and hauled it behind him up the steps to the front porch. At this hour, all was as still as the mouse in that classic Christmas tale Susan loved so much.

His mom opened the door before he could get out his key. He accepted her kiss on his cheek and gave her a squeeze. "Susan asleep?"

"Yes, finally. I had to read that story three times before she conked out." She shut the door behind him and took his rolling case in hand. "I'll put this in your room.

Why don't you go check on her?"

"Might as well. I won't sleep a wink until I do."

He took off his shoes and padded barefoot down the hall. The moment he opened Susan's door, she snapped on the small lamp. "Daddy!"

"Hey, punkin'." He sat on the edge of the bed and gathered her into his arms. "I thought you'd be asleep so Santa could come."

She pushed back her long golden curls and tilted her head like a princess surveying an errant knight. "Gramma doesn't do the voices like you." She leaned back in his arms, and reached over for her book on the nightstand. "You read it, Daddy. Then it will feel like Christmas and Santa will come."

"You got it. You get snuggled in. Where's your doll? We don't want Marylou to miss the story."

Susan felt around the bed and pulled out the floppy cloth doll, propping her up beside her. "There, now she can see the pictures and everything."

"All right, are you ladies ready?" He opened the book.

"Ready." Susan bobbed the doll's head for her.

"T'was the night before Christmas..."

Susan was asleep before he finished the book, but Marylou still sat at attention. He finished the story, playing the part of Santa with a gruff *Ho, ho, ho*, and being the squeaky mouse snoring as he slept in his mouse-house.

"...And to all, a good-night."

Scott leaned over and kissed Susan's cheek, then picked up Marylou, gave her a peck on the head, and snuggled her up against Susan. After tucking the covers around them both, he turned off the light and tiptoed to the door. He shut it quietly.

In his old room, Scott stripped out of his uniform and put on sweatpants and slippers. On his bed was the loose T-shirt with a blond-haired elf on the front that his mother had given him the year before. The elf was shirtless, wearing red boxer shorts with holly on them, and he was licking a candy cane while dangling a round ornament on one finger of his other hand.

Upon seeing the shirt when Scott unwrapped it, a cousin had started singing, *"Don we now our gay apparel..."* and had broken into riotous laughter. That didn't stop the family from insisting he wear it. He was sure he'd asked Mary to give it to Goodwill, so how it had shown up again this year he couldn't explain. Yet, there it was. It could only have come from one person.

"The things we do for our mothers." Scott slipped it on over his head and headed for the kitchen.

He leaned against the door jamb, enjoying the sight. His mother was chopping things for the stuffing and adding them to her biggest bowl. His dad sat at the end of the counter, reading a *Popular Science* magazine. Neither seemed to pay attention to the other, but while his mother was cooking, Dad always kept her company. She'd crochet in a wooden rocker in the garage while he worked on the boat he was building. As if they couldn't bear to be parted from one another, even though they didn't talk much. Maybe they didn't need words.

Scott had thought he and his wife would be the same, but he and Mary had shared a different lifestyle. Both were often busy, and sometimes saw each other only in passing. He'd worked nights, and she'd worked days. She'd had a downtown office, working as an architect for government housing. Time spent outdoors had given her a great tan, but exposed her to hazardous toxins no one had known were in the old buildings being demolished. When she fainted at work, the company sent her in for a check up. After the diagnosis, the project had been shut down immediately, but cancer took a quick toll. Mary was gone in six months. A government investigation into the cause was still ongoing.

Scott now had sole custody of a four-year old daughter and a job that took him into danger every day. He'd shifted to the downtown beat and day shift because it seemed safer, and he could still do what he loved doing: Helping people.

"Well," his dad said, not looking up from his magazine, "Are you going to help your mother or stand there in that dumb elf shirt?"

His mother braced both hands on the counter. "That shirt cost more money than any three pairs of your pants."

"Did not. I paid a pretty penny for these pants."

"Pants were cheaper back in 1982."

He snorted, and went back to his reading.

His mother gave a satisfied nod. "That shirt was custom-made. I wanted it to look like Scott and they did a wonderful job."

Scott drew the shirt away from his body. *This is supposed to be me?* He met his dad's bemused gaze and they both gave that short, man-to-man shrug that meant "women."

His dad went back to reading. His mother continued chopping.

"Mom, I'm ready to work. Tell me what to do."

She dried her hands on her apron and patted his cheek. "Such a good boy you turned out to be."

"Man," his dad interrupted, not looking up.

"Whatever. Scott knows what I mean. His help is a blessing, and it's-- my heavens, look at the time. Did you have to work late?"

He pulled up a stool and told them how he'd met Dara, reminded them about Christine being in Susan's class, and what the guys at the station had helped him do. He left out the part about the romance novels, but explained he'd invited Dara and her daughter to dinner.

His dad put down the magazine and listened, a glimmer of tears in his eyes. "Your mother's right. You are a good man."

"Thanks, Dad."

"I'm glad you invited them." His mom got out more vegetables to dice and chop. "I'll look her up in the phone book and call her in the morning. I want her to know she's welcome."

"Phone book?" His dad snapped open his magazine. "Do they still have such things? I thought these days you had to look people up in Tweeter or Facepad."

"Uh, Dad." Scott pulled out his phone. "It's Twitter and Facebook, and I already have her phone number. Here, Mom. Write this down." He handed it to her. "And yes, there are still phone books for people who want them."

His mother recorded it. "I'll call her about ten or so. In case she sleeps in."

"I think that'd be okay, although her daughter's Susan's age. I doubt she does any more sleeping than I do. Especially Christmas morning."

"Here, son." His mother gave back the phone. "Does she have any family?"

"From what we could tell at the precinct, no living relatives. Husband didn't either. Her Christmas tree was green paper, taped to the wall. Made me not take things for granted, you know?" Their tree, a seven foot fir loaded with lights and ornaments, filled one corner of the front room. "You want me to add an extra leaf to the table?"

"Yes, please, and get out two more of the good plates, and silverware to go with them. Oh, and the platter on top of the hutch. I can't reach it. You know, the one with holly on it."

"If you need help finding it"-- His dad added -- "it looks like the green plant on those boxers your elf is wearing."

Scott sent him a droll stare. "Ha ha."

"Now, Charles," his mother set both hands on her hips. "Stop teasing him. That T-shirt could be a collector's item. There's not another one like it in the world." She resumed her work.

Scott and his dad shared that bemused look again, and Scott set off to do her bidding.

***

Christmas morning, Scott sat on the floor and savored the joy on Susan's face as she opened gifts. Every aunt, uncle, and cousin across the country on both sides of his parents' family had lavished his folks' only grandchild with toys and clothes. She took great pride in modeling each item. After a leisurely breakfast, his mom and dad cleaned up the kitchen, and Scott took Susan outside to ride her new trike. Despite the snow, most of the driveways had been shoveled, and the snow plow had cleared the through streets, so the neighborhood kids were out in force, skating, flying past on bikes, and whizzing by on scooters. All too soon, his little girl would be big enough for a real bike.

He slapped his forehead. "Christine." His wristwatch read 11:38 AM. "Come on, Susan, we need to go inside."

"But, Daddy, I--"

"I have a surprise for you, sweetheart. Come inside."

He ushered her into the house and up to his mom. "I have to pick up certain people. Can you keep an eye on the punkin' here?"

"Sure." His mom kissed him on the cheek. "Better fly."

Grabbing keys, Scott ran to his car. It took a few minutes for the neighborhood kids to get out of the way so he could back out. Outside the subdivision, the roads were almost deserted. He pulled into Dara's driveway a few minutes early.

Scott skipped up the steps and knocked on the door. Jingling keys in his pocket, he whistled while he waited.

* * * *

Dara opened the door to greet Scott. "It was nice of your mother to call me this morning."

"She wanted to make sure you knew you were welcome." He rubbed his hands together. "I hope you're hungry."

"Famished." She took a step closer to Scott and lowered her voice. "And starved for adult conversation. I'm about Barbie'd out."

Scott laughed. "I say let them pick on someone their own size."

"I'm for that. Christine!" she called over her shoulder. "Susan's daddy's here."

Let's go."

Christine stood still as Dara helped her put on her coat and zip it shut. Once done, the little girl launched herself at Scott and he stooped to pick her up in his arms.

"Hi, Mr. Susan's Daddy. I 'member you had cookies at school for Susan's birthday. I ate a pink one."

"Was it good?"

"Uh huh." She patted his face. "Your face feels like my Daddy's."

Scott glanced at Dara.

"Jack didn't shave on weekends until after lunch sometimes."

"Ah. Did he do this, too?" He rubbed his nose against hers, making her giggle.

She put both hands on his cheeks and leaned back to look at him. "That tickles."

"Susan likes it when I do that." He winked at her. "Were you good? What did Santa bring you?"

"Oh, I got toys and books and a dog this big!" She spread her arms.

Scott shared a grin with her mother. "Do you need help carrying anything, Dara?"

"No, I think we're good." She pulled on her coat, Scott helping with one hand while he held her daughter. "I'll grab my purse and the pie."

"Pie? There's pie?" He made sniffing noises.

"I told your mother I'd already baked a peach pie for tomorrow, and talked her into letting me bring it." She retrieved the plastic-wrapped dish from the kitchen.

"You know what, Christine?" Scott adjusted her against his hip. "Susan got a Barbie doll for Christmas. Did you get one, too?"

She bobbed her head. "And her clothes and shoes, and a suitcase for her and everything!"

He set her down. "Why don't you go get yours so you and Susan can play Barbie together?"

Her daughter's endearing blue-eyed gaze lifted to Dara's face. "Mommy, can I?"

"Yes, you may."

Christine bolted for her room.

Dara laid a hand on Scott's arm. "Thank you so much for doing this."

He pressed his hand over hers, his touch sending warm tingles over her skin. *How long has it been since a man touched me, other than to shake hands?* He smelled like clean soap, a hint of leather, and a deeper, masculine scent that was his alone. She leaned in closer to the tantalizing scent.

Scott spread a hand over his chest and grimaced, his cheeks darkening. "It's the shirt, right? I forgot I had it on."

"I'm sorry?"

"You weren't looking at... Oh. Good. Never mind." He zipped up the jacket.

Dara caught a glimpse of an elf image. "It can't be that bad. Show me." She gestured. "Come on. Let me see. You have to take off that jacket sometime."

He rolled his eyes but unzipped the jacket and opened it. "I hate to admit this but I slept in it. I finished putting the trike together late and..." He shrugged.

When she got a look at the blond elf licking a candy cane and wearing red boxer shorts, Dara started laughing, unable to stop herself. She cleared her throat.

"Sorry," she squeaked. A giggle broke out that she couldn't hold inside. "He-- He kind of looks like you."

Scott zipped the jacket shut.

"Let me guess. From either your mom or your sister."

"I don't have a sister, but what made you guess that?"

"It's the kind of shirt a mother or sibling who loves to tease you would give. I think he's cute, and I'd wear him in a heartbeat."

"No kidding? You like my elf?"

"He's adorable."

"You can have him. I'll wash this shirt myself and deliver it tomorrow. I hope the guys at the station don't see me. They'd tease me forever."

"I'm ready," Christine interrupted. "I named my doll Shanika. See?" She held up the Barbie. "I sit by Shanika at school. She's nice. Can we go now?" She took Scott's hand.

"Sure thing. I'm ready for some fun. How about you?" He walked them down to the car and buckled Christine into a booster seat. "This is where Susan sits. She can see the road from here. Do you have a seat like this?"

"Uh huh. I'm a big girl now."

Scott opened the door for Dara. That dimple in his chin showed, and his eyes twinkled. "Need any help?"

"Oh, no. I'm a big girl, too."

When he laughed, the sound reached down into her soul and lingered like a warm hug.

Scott got in and fastened up, then twisted to look at Christine over his shoulder. "I was going to take us home by way of the North Pole, but Santa's elves are all busy cleaning the sleigh, so there's not much to see. Hold on, ladies. Next stop, the Gregori house. With all these kids flying down the road on new bikes, it might take us a couple days."

"Mommy," Christine said. "Mr. Susan's Daddy is so silly. I like him."

Dara shared a smile with Scott. "I do, too." She leaned back in the seat, her heart at rest knowing Christine would spend the day with a friend, having Christmas dinner with a family. Every holiday should be this good.

The blocks of houses rolled by, filled with front yards full of kids playing with new bikes and trikes, and adults tossing footballs and kicking soccer balls with their sons and daughters. Jack would've been out there, pushing Christine on a new bike, or teaching her to throw sticks for the new puppy they'd discussed before-- With resolve, Dara turned her thoughts to the present.

"Here we are." Scott pulled into a long, circular driveway with a ranch-style house at the end. Trees shaded the property. A shed squatted beside the garage on the right. "I grew up here. Christine, see that swing set over there?" He pointed as he pulled the car in under the carport.

"Uh huh. Can I play on it?"

"You and Susan can come out together and I'll push you on the swings right before dinner. If it's okay with your mom."

Christine clapped her hands. "Mommy, can I?"

"I think that would be fun."

Scott came around to open doors for them, Dara first. "Mary was my girlfriend in high school, and she'd come over to do homework. Afterward, we'd sit on the swings and talk. My mother left the kitchen light on so we could 'see what we were doing.'" He helped Christine out of the car. "Might as well have been a spotlight."

"My parents left the porch light on and Jack's mother had a string of white lights in the back yard for parties. They weren't too subtle, were they?"

"Shoot, no. Mary's dad had a big bulldog he'd let outside and that thing would sit right in front of us and stare. Every time I'd try to put my arm around Mary, he'd curl his lip and snarl. Mary joked once that I married her to get rid of Pester. Tell you what, that dog was well named."

The front door opened and a couple came out, the woman in an apron-covered red dress and the man in a red flannel shirt with a white dishcloth over his shoulder. His resemblance to Scott showed in his strong jaw and mouth, a bit of blond hair still showing through the grey; but Scott had gotten his brown eyes and quick smile from his mother.

Welcomes ensued. The pie was offered, and admired. Susan came bouncing out and hugged Christine, giggling and exclaiming about tea sets, Barbies, and stuffed dogs. The adults followed the girls inside.

A massive fir tree filled one corner of the room, hung with bright glass ornaments and strung with garland and lights. The scent of the tree filled the room. Dara drew it in, savoring the familiar smell.

"Your tree is beautiful. It's perfect."

"Thank you." Scott's dad slid his hands into his pockets and surveyed it. "This is one of the best we've found. It's an art. You don't want any bare spots."

Beside him, Scott stood in almost the same pose. He had his dad's chin, and his mother's nose. "Dad and I go to this tree farm over in Hilldale. We couldn't pass this one up. Found a bird's nest inside when we got it home."

"Supposed to be a sign of good luck." Scott's mother asked for Dara's coat and hung it in the closet. "Would you like some tea? I have a good pumpkin spice."

"Yes, thank you, Mrs. Gregori."

"Call me Frances, dear."

"Thank you. I go by Dara, but it's my middle name. My grandmother was named Francie, after her grandmother, who was Frances."

"Was she?" That ready smiled showed itself. "How about that? Frances is a good name."

"I'm Charles." Scott's father shook her hand, pausing to pat it with his other hand. "We're glad to have you here today. I hope you'll make yourself right at home. Now, you have a seat. I'm going to poke this fire a little bit and see if I can get it going again." He picked up a poker and began adjusting the logs with it.

"Mom?" Scott followed the woman into the kitchen. "Anything I can do to help?"

"Thank you, sweetie, but everything's fine for now. I'm putting the teapot on, but the table's all set, the pecan pie is done, the turkey's on its last round of basting, and all the sides are warming in the bottom oven. Last things to do are biscuits and gravy, and we'll be ready to eat."

Scott returned and sat beside Dara. "Mom has a double oven. She loves to bake."

"Bet she can tell that by looking at me." Scott's father eased into a rocker.

She smiled at him. "Frances, I can help with those biscuits if you need it. My gravy is... well, let's just say it's 'Do you want one lump, or two?' But I can make pie crust to die for, and my biscuits are so tender they hardly need butter."

"Now there's an offer I won't refuse. When it's time, you're on. And I can teach you how to make gravy. I know a trick or two."

"You've got a deal."

Charles adjusted a pillow behind him. "What kind of work do you do, Dara?"

"I bill insurance for a hospital. It's a tough, thankless job, but it saves our patients so much hassle. Now that I've been a patient there, I'm doubly glad for the staff in that department. They were wonderful. What do you do?"

"I'm retired, but I was a carpenter for more than forty years. Built most of the furniture in this house." He swept a hand around the room. "Hutch in the dining room, table and chairs, counters and cupboards in the kitchen. All the beds."

"He even did the mantle around the fireplace. He's so talented." Scott's mother set a tray on the small table. A lovely china tea set filled it, morning glories glowing from every surface. "Here we are. Scott, why don't you pour?" She sat in the other rocker, near her husband.

"This is beautiful." Dara caressed the handle of the pot. "I've never seen a teapot with such vibrant color."

"Thank you. It was my mother's. It was handmade in England when she and my dad were stationed there. A little out-of-the-way tea shop right below their flat. Dad was an officer in the Army, and my mother helped out in the shop a few days every week. They couldn't pay her much, but the owner made her that set as a gift before my folks came back to the States. I cherish it. They're both gone now. I bring it out every holiday."

Dara accepted the brimming tea cup Scott handed her. "What a lovely way to honor them." The pumpkin spice tea held its own sweetness, the heat perfect. She took a long sniff of the rich fragrance, then another sip. "Mmm. This is delicious. Thank you so much. It's a pleasure to be here today."

The four adults paused now and again to check on the girls, who were having their own tea party with pretend tea, their Barbies guests at a tiny table. Both of the girls wore hats and gloves, the fingertips a bit too long, and each had a feather boa around her neck. It did Dara's heart good to see her daughter having such fun. How would she ever get her to leave when it was time?

Scott and his dad took the girls outside to the swings while Dara helped Frances put together the last bits of dinner. Working beside her in the warm kitchen felt right. They moved around one another as if they'd cooked together every day. Frances talked about Scott as a boy, and Dara hung on every word. He'd been a track all-star, varsity basketball player, and a good student. His mother teared up suddenly, and then shook her head.

"He's a good man, my Scott. This last year has been hard on him. First Mary being sick, and then--" Frances took off her apron. "Enough of the past. Today's been good. I was worried how he'd handle Christmas. I haven't seen him this happy in a long time."

Before Dara could think what to say, the men came back inside with the girls. A flurry of activity followed, with coats being hung up and hands being washed.

When they sat down at the table to eat, it felt natural to hold hands with Scott on one side and Christine on the other during the blessing. Scott's father did the honors, and it was short, earnest, and thankful. Afterward, he clapped his hands like a boy.

"Now, who's hungry?" He stood and set about carving the turkey.

For a small family, there was enough food to feed two armies. Turkey, stuffing, both mashed and sweet potatoes, fresh cranberry relish, green bean casserole (Dara's favorite), beets, zucchini, and of course, melt-in-your-mouth biscuits and gravy. For once, Christine didn't turn up her nose at the beets, probably because Susan took a big helping.

Dinner passed all too quickly. The food was heavenly, and the turkey every bit as moist and amazing as Scott had sworn. By the end, both girls started dozing in their chairs.

Dara leaned back, so full she couldn't have forced another bite. "Looks like I need to take my little one home and put her in bed."

"No, you can't go home yet." Scott stood and pushed in his chair. "We haven't had pie. We can put the girl's on Susan's bed, and after their nap, we'll have dessert."

She swallowed, fighting joyful tears at not having to leave this warm, loving haven. Dara nodded, and got up to help him.

Chapter Three

Scott and Dara carried the girls into Susan's room and put them on the double bed, then stood side by side, watching them sleep.

Scott leaned one hand against the wall. "They look alike. Blonde hair, big smiles, and they get along like sisters."

"They do."

He tucked a blanket around the girls. "I always wanted a brother to play with."

"I always wished for a sister."

"So we're both only children with only children."

"I guess we are." Dara tidied the tea set. "I was raised in foster care. My parents were killed in a car accident when I was ten. I swung from anger to terror and back. When Jack died, I was terrified of something happening to me. Then I had the accident. My first thought was what if Christine ended up the same way, with no one. I didn't think I'd ever get a handle on my fear."

"Did you?"

"I'm still working on it, but yeah. It's happening more each day. Jack had insisted we each have a will, and we had insurance. When he died, it paid off our house and car, and a bit more. I was grateful for his foresight. One thing I've learned though. Whatever you think is good enough isn't. Still, it was more than my parents did for me. They were young when they died. Early thirties. I imagine they thought they'd live forever. I'm sure you know what I'm talking about."

"Do I! Once we knew Mary was ill, it was too late to get insurance. We always thought we'd have time. Plus, in my job... You'd think we'd know better, but we were always so busy, and then it was too late." He shook his head. "But enough about death. It's Christmas, and that's about life. Let's think about that." Scott nodded toward the door. "It's a beautiful day. What do you say we bundle up and go sit on the swings?"

She thought of his parents leaving the lights on so she and Scott would be able to "see." It was early, and while darkness was falling, it was still light.

She nodded. "I'd like that."

Wrapped in warm parkas and with a plaid woolen blanket to share, they headed out to the swings. On one end, a short, two-seater had been hung for Scott's parents. That way they could be outside with Susan, but not have to stand the entire time.

Scott settled into the seat and rested his arm across the back, inviting Dara to join him. Once she did, he tossed the blanket across their legs. The small swing meant their bodies touched, from hips to thighs.

Dara held her breath for a moment, but as Scott began to swing them, gently, one booted toe on the ground, she relaxed.

"Comfy?"

She hadn't been this comfy in years. "Yes. This is nice."

The light from the porch bathed the yard, and light from the kitchen window framed their seat.

"I should have helped your mother do the dishes." But Dara didn't move.

"Dad likes to help her. Now, if she's cooking, he'll sit there and read, but he likes the sudsy water. When I was first engaged to Mary, he had me come help him in the kitchen and told Mom to go relax with her soon to be daughter-in-law. You know what he told me?"

She tilted back her head. His dark eyes weren't visible in the changing twilight, but his bright smile shone. "What?"

"That the best sex always begins in the kitchen."

Dara giggled, covering her mouth. "What?"

"He said if a man takes the same responsibility as his wife does in dealing with cleaning up the kitchen, and getting the kids in bed then she'll know he values her.

She'll feel loved." He nodded toward the window. "See?"

His dad was leaning over to give his mother a peck on the cheek, and she wrapped her arms around his neck and kissed him back.

She sighed. "Oh, that's so sweet."

"Used to embarrass the heck out of me when my friends came over, till I found out they all wished their folks were like mine."

The light in the kitchen window winked out. The yard fell into darkness except for a band of light on the porch. A moment later, it went out as well.

Neither Dara nor Scott moved. They sat together on the swing, hanging on to the moment, savoring the privacy.

"Wow," Scott said. "That's never happened before." He patted his coat pockets. "No worries. I have my keys."

"Keys?"

"To get in. Maybe they forgot we were out here."

Dara turned her head, hiding her smile. Sure they did. Or were Scott's parents giving a kind of blessing?

Scott dug in with his boot toe again, pushing the swing. "We're safe in the dark. Plenty of moonlight and it's a good neighborhood."

She relaxed against him, enjoying his warmth. "Do the neighbors know you're a cop?"

"Oh sure."

"Well, there you go." She smiled up at him. "I'm plenty safe."

They sat in companionable silence. The stars overhead shone in all their brilliant splendor. A television played the opening music from *It's a Wonderful Life.* Soft sounds of nature intruded, a pine cone dropping, the *plop* of snow clumps falling off the trees. An owl hooted in the distance.

The words Scott's mother shared came back to her. *"I haven't seen him this happy in a long time."*

Dara hadn't been this happy in a long time, either. Would it last?

"You know," Scott began, "I'd like to take you out to dinner in a few days, if it's okay. Christine could come over and play with Susan. I'll clear it with mom, but I'm sure she'll say yes."

"Or I can ask my friend, Sherilyn, to keep the girls."

"So, that's a yes? You'll go?"

"Yeah." Dara crossed her ankles. "I'd like to get to know you."

"Good. I know I'm just a cop, but I--"

"'Just' a cop?" Dara sat up straighter. "Hey, never apologize for that. You are not 'just' a cop. You're not 'just' anything." Dara nudged aside the lapel of his coat so the elf on his shirt showed. "A guy who wears a shirt like this to please his mom, spends the day playing with kids and helping others..." She met his gaze. "I'm definitely interested in getting to know a man like that."

Pride beamed in Scott's smile, and it shot little tingles down Dara's spine.

Her heart felt settled, calm, and yet eager at the same time. As a single mom, she'd resigned herself to being alone, and now... Did she dare to hope there might be more?

Scott let out a long, sighing breath. "It's good to be with someone who knows what I'm going through. Being a single dad... it's work. I haven't had the energy, or the interest, in getting to know anyone."

"Same here. You're lucky to have your folks. My best friend has been a godsend. I couldn't have made it without Sherilyn and her husband. They've been wonderful with Christine."

"Maybe we have more in common, beside our girls, and our loss. Maybe by Christmas next year, we'll be back here sitting on this same swing. I don't know." He dragged a hand through his hair. "But I like you and Christine. I think we have a shot at something. I want to find out. I'm not one to rush things. I want us both to be sure. For our sake, and for our daughters. It's important to me that Susan never forget her mother. At the same time, I don't want to be alone. I don't think Mary would want me to be. She'd want Susan and me to be happy."

"Jack would want the same for us. Christine and I talk about her daddy every chance we get. With you, I don't have to pretend everything's fine. That there's not still pain. It's getting better, but some days it's hard. You know?"

"I do indeed." Scott looked down at her. He was quiet, his gaze steady. "What do you say? Shall we give this a go? Do you think it's worth taking time to see where we are in a year?" He took her hand in his, and Dara leaned against him.

"Scott, to me, that sounds like the best Christmas ever."

THE END
* * * *

About the Author

Kayelle Allen is a multi-published, EPIC Award winning author. She writes Contemporary Romance, Science Fiction, Science Fiction Romance, Mainstream Fantasy, Gay Romance, and non-fiction. She likes to attend Science Fiction conventions, and has been a speaker at DragonCon, and Gaylaxicon. She holds an honorary lifetime membership at OutlantaCon. Kayelle is the founder of the author-mentoring group Marketing for Romance Writers, and manages the successful Romance Lives Forever blog. She is a US Navy Veteran, and founded the graphics and eBook conversion company The Author's Secret. Kayelle is married to her personal hero, and makes her home in the southeast.

Books by Kayelle Allen

Links to buy all books http://kayelleallen.com/Books.html
Like an autograph for this book? http://authorgraph.com/authors/kayelleallen
Get one email when Kayelle's next book releases.
http://authoralarms.com/Kayelle_Allen

Contacting Kayelle

You can reach Kayelle Allen via email at kayelle.allen@yahoo.com

Social Media

Website http://kayelleallen.com
Blog (Unstoppable Heroes) http://kayelleallen.com/blog
Twitter http://twitter.com/kayelleallen
Facebook author page http://facebook.com/kayelleallen.author/
G+ https://plus.google.com/u/0/106709321860454955924/posts
Pinterest http://pinterest.com/kayelleallen/
DeviantArt http://kayelleallen.deviantart.com/
Goodreads http://goodreads.com/KayelleAllen
Shelfari http://shelfari.com/kayelleallen

Paper.li Newsletters Published by Kayelle

A Writer's Business http://paper.li/kayelleallen/1318689164
DIKY (Don't I Know You? Celebrities on Twitter) http://paper.li/kayelleallen/1376665169
Hottest Writers on the Web http://paper.li/kayelleallen/1345939402
Loki's Army Recruiters http://paper.li/kayelleallen/1383533309
Marketing for Romance Writers Org http://paper.li/kayelleallen/1340913374
New Books Every Day (Rated R) http://paper.li/kayelleallen/1337982138
Romance Lives Forever http://paper.li/kayelleallen/1349530261
Tribe Mates: A Triberr Gathering http://paper.li/kayelleallen/1324406942

Formatting in this book

Formatting in this book is by The Author's Secret, supporting authors with affordable eBook conversions, editing, custom and ready made book covers, graphic design, and more. Privately owned and staffed by professional authors, editors, and artists. https://theauthorssecret.com

Before You Say Good-bye...

You have the opportunity to review this book and share your thoughts on Facebook and Twitter. If you believe the story has value and is worth sharing, would you take a few seconds to let your friends know about it? If it turns out they like it, they'll be grateful to you. As will I.

Made in the USA
Lexington, KY
18 November 2014